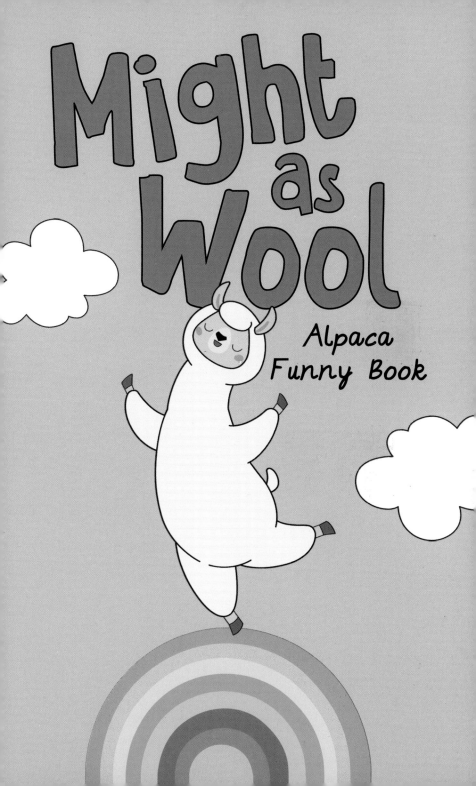

All rights reserved. Published by Scholastic Inc., *Publishers since 1920.* SCHOLASTIC and associated logos are trademarks and/or registered trademarks of Scholastic Inc. The publisher does not have any control over and does not assume any responsibility for author or third-party websites or their content.

No part of this publication may be reproduced, stored in a retrieval system, or transmitted in any form or by any means, electronic, mechanical, photocopying, recording, or otherwise, without written permission of the publisher. For information regarding permission, write to Scholastic Inc., Attention: Permissions Department, 557 Broadway, New York, NY 10012.

This book is a work of fiction. Names, characters, places, and incidents are either the product of the author's imagination or are used fictitiously, and any resemblance to actual persons, living or dead, business establishments, events, or locales is entirely coincidental.

ISBN 978-1-338-71753-2

10 9 8 7 6 5 4 3 2   21 22 23 24 25

Printed in the U.S.A.   40

First printing 2021

Illustrations by Artful Doodlers Ltd.
Book design by Elliane Mellet

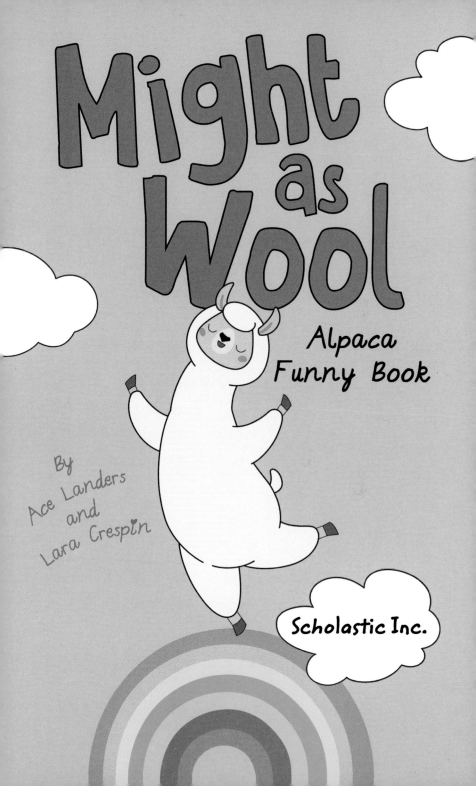

My name is Alpaca. I live in **ALPACALANDIA.** You can call me Allie. Or Al. Or whatever you wish!

But something you should never, ever, EVER call me is a llama. EVER.

Okay? Got it? **GOOD**.

ALPACAS

-Adorable, small ears

-Soft, fluffy fur

-Average height:
35 inches

-Herd-based animals
(we LOVE teamwork)

-Smart! Funny!
Amazing!

-Allowed in
Alpacalandia

Nothing.
And don't you
fur-get it!

LLAMAS

- Giant, banana-shaped ears

- Coarse, double-layered fur

- Average height: 45 inches

- Independent (not good at teamwork)

- Horrible! Will spit in your face! The worst!

- NOT allowed in Alpacalandia

Alpacas are special creatures.
We come from the camel family,
but we aren't camels. They have humps.

SEE?

There's lots that alpacas like to do.
I spend my days:

HUMMING,

GRAZING,

AND HERDING SHEEP.

When I was a wee little alpaca, I became best friends with a girl named El. But soon she moved to a place called San Fleece-isco.

El and I write letters to each other, just like real pen pals! El knows me better than anyone.

DID YOU KNOW?!

A baby alpaca is called a "cria."

A baby llama is called a "cria," too, but we don't talk about that . . .

All About El

El ♥

El

Favorite Food:
Banana Spit

Favorite Color:
Mahogan-hay

Favorite Book:
Winnie-the-Paca

Favorite Movie:
Hairy Paw-ter and the Order of the Alpaca

CINEMA TICKET

HAIRY PAW-TER AND THE ORDER

A23

4 APR   18:00

5 USD   00123456789 7

Favorite Quote:

"Where there's a will, there's a hay!"

El and I talk about everything.
We have all the same interests, like . . .

AL AND EL'S
FAVORITE CELEBRITIES

Tail-or
Swift

Britney
Shears

Ariana
Grazé

Hair-rison
Ford

wool.i.am

Camel-a Cabello

Brad Spit

Meryl Sheep

Ed Shear-an

Weird Al-Paca

AL AND EL'S FAVORITE FOODS

Hum-mus

Paw-sta

Alpaca-dos

Toma-toes

Alpa-candy

Mac-and-fleece

Paw-pcorn

Pota-toes

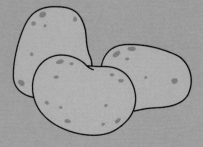

Fur-ench fries

Shep-herd's pie

And, of course, our favorite movies!

AL AND EL'S FAVORITE FLICKS

The Fast &
the Fur-ious

Alpaca-lypse Now

Kung Fu
Alpaca

Fur-ozen

The
Incredi-pacas

ALPACAS, INC.

Alpacas, Inc.

Alpaca-Man:
Fur from Home

The Rise of
Sky-whisker

THE BEAUTY & THE LLAMA

The Beauty and
the Llama

De-spit-able
Me

19

But I haven't seen El since we were little.

I don't even know what she looks like now.

Which gives me a **BRILLIANT** idea!

I'll go to San Fleece-isco!

El and I will have the best time ever
doing all kinds of things!

WHAT I'M AL-PACKING

A camel-ra

A gnaw-vel

My wool-et

My reusable
water paw-tle

An i.Pawd

San Fleece-isco is a little far from Alpacalandia. I have to take . . .

a car,

a train,

a bus,

and an al-plane!

BUT THEN I ARRIVE!

WHOA.
San Fleece-isco sure is **BIG**.

29

El lives somewhere by the beach.
I can't wait to see her. It's going to be

ALPACA-MAZING!

But wait!
She doesn't know
I'm coming. I should
get her a gift.

I never knew a shop could have so many things. I hate to admit it. I'm . . . overwoolmed!

So I get a new idea.
I'm going to sing El a song. It'll be . . .

But when I arrive at the address
on El's letters, something feels off.
It smells like . . . llama?

And there are llama footprints, too!

Uh-oh. This can't be good. This is very, very, very not good. It can only mean one thing:

EL'S HOUSE HAS BEEN INVADED BY LLAMAS.

"Don't worry, El! I'll come rescue you!"

I'm right.

There, sitting in the inside of El's house, like it belongs there, is a big, stinkin', mean, nasty . . .

LLAMA!

"Al, is that you?" the llama asks.

"How do you know my name?" I ask.

The horrible llama stands up.

"I'm El," she says. "Well, actually, it's L. It's short for Llama. I left Alpacalandia because everyone hates llamas there. And I didn't want any prob-llamas!"

My head is spinning.
El is a llama?

This must be the
ALPACALYPSE.

"I'm sorry I mislead you," El says. "But I only ever wanted to be your fur-end. And I thought, if you didn't know I was a llama, there'd be no drama!"

I had no idea that El was a llama.
But looking into her eyes, her big ol' llama
eyes, near her big ol' llama ears, I realize
something. She's still my best fur-end.

"THIS IS A LLAMA TO HANDLE," I say.

"It's okay," El says. "I'm really glad to see ewe, Al! And if you can get past me being a llama, there's a lot of fun things to do in San Fleece-isco."

"Well . . ." El says.
"We can go to the swimming paw-l!"

El and I put on our bathing suits.

POOL RULES:
- NO HORSING AROUND
- NO CHICKEN FIGHTING
- NO SWAN DIVING
- ENJOY THE KITTY POOL
- NO MONKEY BUSINESS

I guess you might as wool . . .

El in her bathing suit and Al with their floatie

put the
COOL in **POOL!**

POOL JOKES,
by Al and El

Why can elephants swim anytime they want?

They always have their **trunks** on!

What did the ocean say to the pool?

Nothing, but it **waved**!

Why do sheep love to swim?

Because they can **baaaa**ckstroke!

Who cleans the pool?

Mer-**maids**!

49

Next, we go camping.

San Fleece-isco has a great camping spot.

When you're camping, you might as wool . . .

stop and smell the flowers.

El teaches me all her favorite llama jokes, too.

What's a llama's favorite thing to say in Spanish?

¿Cómo te llamas? (It means "What's your name?")

How does a llama wake up in the morning?

With its a-llama!

What's a llama's favorite drink?

Llamanade!

What's a llama's favorite place to visit?

Australi-ama!

How does a llama singer prepare for her big debut?

La, la, llama!

B-E-E

What's more unbelievable than a talking llama?

A spelling bee!

What do you do when you want to preserve a piece of paper?

You llamanate it!

What's a llama's favorite way to travel?

In a llama-sine!

Then she tells me about her favorite celebri-llamas!

Kendrick Llamar

The Dalai Llama

Rillama

Se-llama Gomez

Llama del Rey

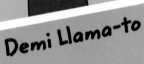
Demi Llama-to

Doja Llama

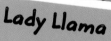
Lady Llama

Post Mallama

Llama-donna

We come up with a list of all our favorite things!

My favorite holiday?

FLEECE NAVIDAD!

El's favorite holiday?

HAPPY LLAMA-KAH!

Of course, there's other great holidays too, like

RAM-ADAN,

MARDI BAA,

and

DI-WOOL-I!

My favorite superhero is . . .

IRON-PACA!

El's favorite superhero is . . .

CAP-LLAMA!

While we're visiting a llama-brary, I get an idea.

El looks
A-LLAMA-ED!

"I can't go back to Alpacalandia, Al," she says. "They don't like llamas. Remember?"

"But I think we could change things! Make everyone see how great you really are!"

"And what if they like me? Will they put in the work to treat me like an equal?"

I don't have an answer.
El tells me it's time I
should go back home.

A-llama-one.

When I arrive back home, I try to do the same things I always did.

I try to have an alpaca-nic,

sing alpaca-pella,

listen to mu-spit,

and eat paw-sta.

But none of it feels right. I miss El.

I used to love Alpacalandia. But how can I love a place that won't welcome my best friend?

Then I get an idea.

Mayor Alpaca cries.
My plan must have failed.

"My best friend is a llama, too!"
Mayor Alpaca shouts. "But I thought
she'd never be wool-come here."

Whoa. I did not see that coming!

There's bustling in the crowd.

"My best friend
is a Shiba Inu,"
says another
alpaca.

"Mine is a frog!"

"A pigeon!"

"A potbelly pig!"

"A dragon!"

We take it to a vote, and it's
un-animal-ous!

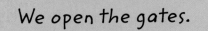

We open the gates.

Our first visitor is a bear.

"What do you call a bear with no teeth?"
he asks.

A GUMMY BEAR!

The next visitor is a crocodile.

What do you call a gator in a vest?

AN INVESTI-GATOR!

What do you call a fish without an eye?

A FSH!

What's a snake's favorite school subject?

HISS-TORY!

It's **AWESOME** that there are so many visitors in Alpacalandia. But there's someone missing . . .

"Thank you for making me feel w-EL-comed," El says. "Now, let's get to work! We have to make sure everyone feels safe in Alpacalandia, no matter what."

Everything is better when you do it **TOGETHER!**

After all, you . . .

MIGHT AS